Universal Reference Guide

DINOSAURS

UNIVERSAL REFERENCE GUIDE: **DINOSAURS**

Image courtesy:
Inspirock
Alamy
Stock Photos
iStock
Getty Images

Compiled and edited by: NextStage
Published by: Portrait Library

Edition: 2024

Contents

4
What is a dinosaur?

6
Common features of a dinosaur

8
Land dinosaurs

13
Evolutionary origins

16
Arrangement according to size

18
Behaviour of dinosaurs

20
How they are born?

22
The true story of birds

26
Aquatic dinosaurs

28
The Extinction Level Event or ELE

30
Life after extinction: The Cenozoic Era

31
Depictions of dinosaurs: Early period to present

What is a dinosaur?

Dinosaurs are a diverse group of reptiles classified under a group called Dinosauria. These species first appeared during the Triassic period between 243- 233.23 million years ago, but the exact origin and period of the evolution of dinosaurs is a question many scientists are still trying to answer to this day. They became the dominant species after the Triassic period and continued from the Jurassic through the Cretaceous periods. Fossil records also indicate that birds are modern feathered dinosaurs, having evolved from earlier theropods.

RICHARD OWEN'S CONTRIBUTION TO SCIENCE

The term 'Dinosauria' was first formally coined in 1841 by the paleontologist Sir Richard Owen. It was used in reference to the 'distinct tribe or sub-order of Saurian Reptiles' that were being discovered in England and other parts of the world at that time. The term is a derivation of the Greek word deinos (meaning terrible, potent or fearfully great) and sauros (meaning lizard or reptile). Since then, discoveries from every continent have filled museums with a growing number of unusual dinosaurs. As more and more discoveries are being made everyday, paleontologists are finding it harder and harder to exactly define what makes a dinosaur what it is.

Paleontologists have discovered and categorized over 1000 dinosaurs, with some being 100 feet long and others weighing over 70 tonnes. Broadly speaking, there were horned dinosaurs, armored dinosaurs, dome-headed dinosaurs, crested dinosaurs, sickle-clawed dinosaurs and long neck dinosaurs. Many of them lived an entirely terrestrial life but some had ventured into lakes and rivers, while others took to the skies, becoming the earliest birds the world had ever seen. Recently, scientists were shocked by evidence indicating that an amphibious dinosaur once roamed the lands and seas.

QUICK FACTS

A diapsid means they had two holes in their skull located behind the eyes. This feature helped lighten their skulls and provided important attachment places for facial muscles.

The gigantosaurus is a common example of a bipedal dinosaur

TWO LEGGED OR FOUR LEGGED

Early on, it was thought that all dinosaurs were bipedal. But as time passed and more discoveries were made, paleontologists concluded that some species were quadrupedal and there were those that could shift between the two stances. Further analysis indicated how some species had elaborate displays like horns or crests, while others developed bony armor and spines.

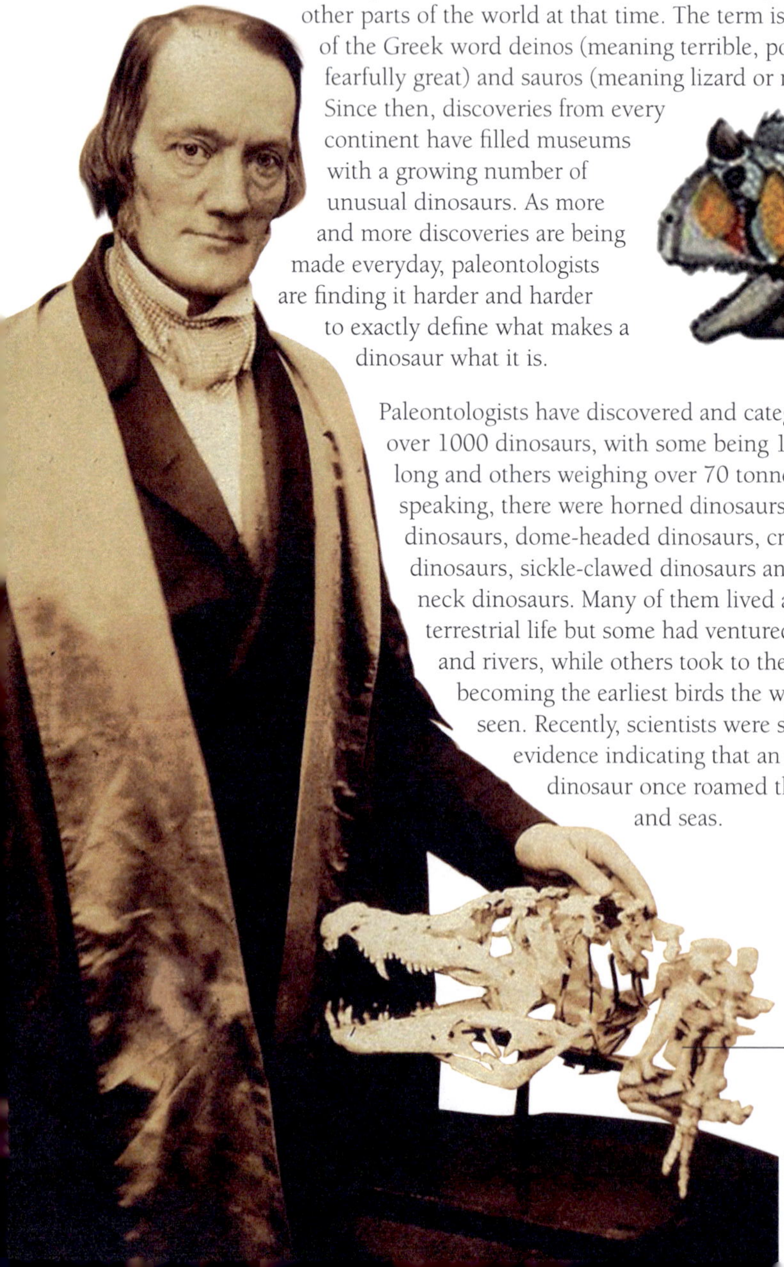

Richard Owen, an English biologist, comparative anatomist, paleontologist with a remarkable gift for interpreting fossils

KINDS OF DINOSAURS

Through phylogenic nomenclature, the term Dinosauria is a combination of both Ornithischia (class of herbivorous dinosaurs) and Saurischia (lizard hipped dinosaurs). It also encompasses ankylosaurians (armored herbivorous quadrupeds), stegosaurians (plated herbivorous quadrupeds), ceratopsians (herbivorous quadrupeds with horns and frills), ornithopods (bipedal or quadrupedal herbivores), theropods (mostly bipedal carnivores and birds) and sauropodomorphs (large herbivorous quadrupeds with long necks and tails).

The Ankylosaurus is a famous example of a quadruped dinosaur

The Megalosaurus is said to be the first dinosaur ever scientifically described. This was done by William Buckland, a British fossil hunter in 1819. In 1824, he described and named them.

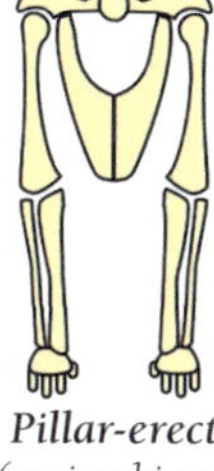

Sprawling

Erect (dinosaurs, mammals)

Pillar-erect (rauisuchians)

SHARED TRAITS

Although recent discoveries make it difficult to have a universally agreed-upon list of distinguishing features for dinosaurs, nearly all the species so far share certain similarities to one another. They all laid and hatched from eggs, they constantly lost and grew teeth, they were vertebrates that shared similar skeletal features, they walked with their legs directly underneath their bodies like birds, they were diapsids and had a similar hip and thigh region. It is this similarity that gave dinosaurs their upright, pillar-legged posture.

Thanks to the above information, it is inferred that dinosaurs were a species with hind limbs held erect beneath the body. There are a number of prehistoric animals that are popularly thought of as dinosaurs. These are ichthyosaurs, mosasaurs, plesiosaurs, pterosaurs and pelycosaurs. Though these animals did look like dinosaurs, from a scientific perspective, none of them had the erect hind limb posture that had become a distinguishing characteristic among true dinosaurs.

DINOSAURS WERE NOT ALONE

When the dinosaurs ruled the planet as the dominant species, they were not the only species living at the time. Due to the atmospheric conditions of Earth millions of years ago, the other groups of animals were restricted in size. Early mammals for example rarely exceeded the size of a domestic cat. These mammals were mostly as small as a rodent and were often prey for much larger carnivores.

THERE WERE MANY DINOSAURS

It is worth noting that dinosaurs have always been an extremely varied group of animals. Based on a study conducted in 2006, over 500 non-avian dinosaur genera have been identified with total certainty so far. The study also shows the total number of genera preserved in the fossil record is estimated to be 1850, of which nearly 75% is yet to be discovered. Another study posits that about 3400 genera of dinosaur existed, which includes many that could not be preserved in the fossil records.

By 2016, paleontologists estimate the number of dinosaur species that lived from the Mesozoic era is estimated to be between 1543 – 2468. Fossils of dinosaurs can be found in every continent, indicating that the species achieved global distribution by at least the early Jurassic period.

QUICK FACTS

The plural of genus is genera.

A symmetrodoni, an example of the earliest mammals to live on Earth

Common features of a dinosaur

Now that it has been established what is a dinosaur, how many there were and some of the simpler distinguishing characteristics, it is time to learn in greater detail the common features that the species shared.

Aside from the features provided earlier on, there are a number of anatomical features that through the years have led paleontologists to conclude which bones belonged to a dinosaur and which did not.

An artistic representation of what a Scythosuchus looked like

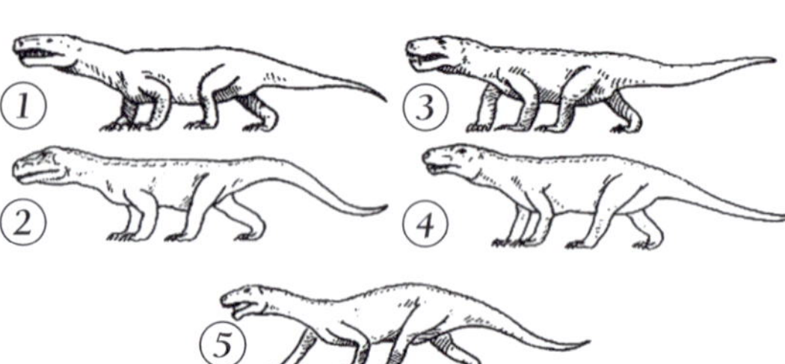

Possible interpretations of what a Tsylmosuchus looked like

QUICK FACTS

Archosaurs are a group of animals whose living representatives consist of birds and crocodilians. While it is difficult to ascertain when the first archosaurs first appeared, modern taxonomists agree that they were first seen during the Early Triassic period. The earliest archosaurs were the Scythosuchus and Tsylmosuchus, whose remains have been found in Russia.The skeleton of Archosaurs is the template from which the dinosaurs and later descendants came from.

WHAT THEY LOOKED LIKE

Paleontologists the world over agree that nearly all discovered dinosaurs at present tend to share certain modifications or similarities to the common Archosauria skeleton, or are direct descendants of older dinosaurs showing these modifications. Later groups of dinosaurs had further modifications to these traits. Such modifications originating in the most recent common ancestor of a certain class of species is called the synapomorphies of such a group. There is a detailed assessment of archosaur interrelations provided by a noted paleontologist that confirm twelve distinguishing characteristics found in dinosaurs.

Most dinosaurs had a scaly skin and no hair on their bodies. While it is easy to think of them as grey, monotone creatures, many experts surmise that some of them could have been colourful. These dinosaurs could have used their colours during mating rituals.

HOT VS COLD

Scientists are often divided over whether dinosaurs were cold or warm-blooded animals. Considering how their descendants (reptiles and birds) are both warm and cold blooded, many experts are hard pressed to find enough evidence to support either theory. The only thing that everyone in the scientific community agree upon is that they had their own way of regulating their body temperature.

Due to their hollow bones, small dinosaurs like the velociraptor could move much faster than regular dinosaurs

FAST AND SLOW

Dinosaurs that were able to walk upright had hollow or light bones, enabling them to move quickly across the land. The larger and heavier dinosaurs had strong bones to support their massive weight. These dinosaurs moved slowly on all four legs.

Through various excavations and fossils, scientists believe this diagram shows what a Silesaurus would have looked like

SKELETAL SIMILARITIES

Experts have also found a number of other possible similarities and discounted a number of synapomorphies suggested earlier on. Some of these traits are also present in silesaurids, which were recategorized as a sister group of Dinosauria. These similarities included a large anterior trochanter, metatarsals II and IV of subequal length, reduced contact between ischium and pubis, the presence of a cnemial crest on the tibia of an ascending process on the astragalus and many others.

Also, a variety of skeletal features are shared by dinosaurs. However, because they are either common to other groups of archosaurs or were not present in early dinosaurs, such features were not seen as synapomorphies. When it came to diapsids for example, dinosaurs had two pairs of temporal fenestrae, and Archosauria had two more openings in the snout and lower jaw. Additionally, further studies revealed how certain characteristics thought to be synapomorphies are now known to have actually appeared before dinosaurs, or were absent in early dinosaurs and then appeared in different dinosaur groups. Some of these synapomorphies include an elongated scapula or shoulder blade, a sacrum made up of three or more fused vertebrae and a perforate acetabulum or hip socket with a hole at the center of its inside surface.

THE WAY THEY WALKED

An important feature of a dinosaur is how they stand. Dinosaurs stand with their hind limbs erect in a way similar to most modern mammals, making its posture distinct from most other reptiles, whose limbs extend out to either side. This posture is caused by the laterally facing recess in the pelvis and a corresponding inwardly facing distinct head on the femur. This posture allowed early dinosaurs to breathe easily while moving around, which permitted stamina and activity levels that greatly surpassed those of 'sprawling' reptiles and prevented Carrier's Constraint. Erect limbs also helped support the evolution of the large size by reducing bending stress on the limbs.

Typical Dinosaur

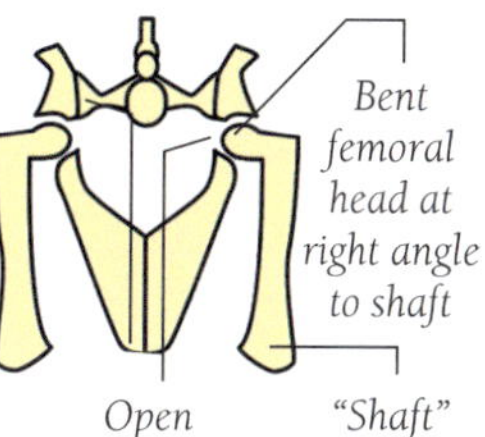

Rauisuchians

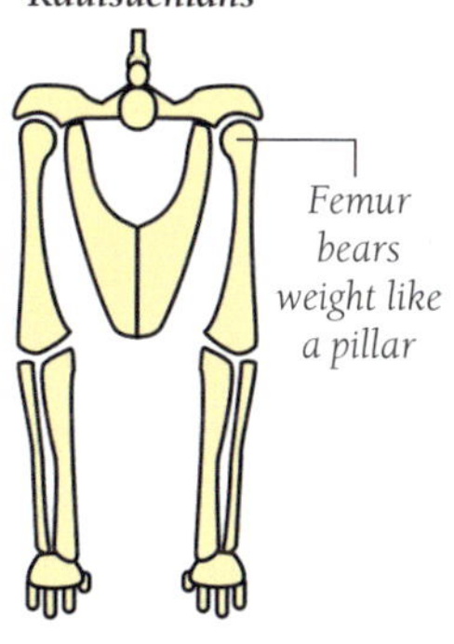

Hip joint configuration in regular dinosaurs show the femur slightly further from the hip but in Rauisuchians, the femurs are much closer together.

Some non-dinosaurian archosaurs, like the rauisuchians also had erect limbs. They did this by a 'pillar erect' configuration of the hip joint, where the upper pelvic bone was rotated to form an overhanging shelf. This was different, as the regular hip joint configuration had a projection from the femur insert on a socket on the hip.

'Carrier's Constraint' is the observation that air-breathing vertebrates having two lungs and flexing their bodies sideways during locomotion, find it difficult to move and breathe at the same time.

As seen in the movies, larger dinosaurs moved slower than regular dinosaurs

AN EARLY ROADBLOCK

An early problem experts faced was the difficulty of determining what features made a dinosaur. This is because early dinosaurs and other archosaurs have many similar features. As such, many animals were misidentified in early literature and records.

QUICK FACTS

A Synapomorphy is a shared or derived character trait common between an ancestor and its descendant.

Land dinosaurs

Dinosaurs, like all living things are grouped together based on their physical features and how closely related they are to one another. Most dinosaurs are best-known by their genus, rather than by their species name. For example, many people know and discuss about the iguanodon, which is a genus and not a specific species. Another good example is the famous dinosaur - the Tyrannosaurus Rex, which is in fact a species of the Tyrannosaurus.

On the whole, dinosaurs are grouped into two types: saurischian and ornithischian. Thanks to English paleontologist, Harry Seeley for this classification, who noticed how one type of dinosaur had hips like a lizard and the other had a bird-like hip structure. Hence, he decided to name them after the Greek words for lizard and bird hip joint.

All carnivorous dinosaurs were saurischian along with many herbivorous dinosaurs. On the other side, all ornithischians were herbivores. There have been recent findings which indicate that some ornithischians were omnivorous or even carnivorous.

Saurischian pelvis

Ilion

Isquion

Pibus

SAURISCHIAN

When it came to saurischian, this group is further divided into theropods and sauropods. Theropod dinosaurs were bipedal meat eaters, with theropod itself being the Greek word for 'wild beast foot.' Theropods were first seen during the late Triassic period and existed all the way till the Cretaceous-Paleogene extinction event.

Interestingly though, theropods were not completely wiped out during this extinction level event. In fact, one such group survived and branched off, eventually evolving into birds. Aside from this, are the various other groups of dinosaurs classified under the Theropod category.

COELUROSAURS

These are a large group of dinosaurs, whose major groups include Carnosaurians and the Tyrannosaurids.

Due to recent scientific discoveries, many paleontologists firmly believe this is what raptors actually looked like

An artistic depiction of what a Maniraptora could have looked like

MANIRAPTORA

They are a branch of bird-like dinosaurs. The group first appeared in the Jurassic period and are seen as the ancestors to modern-day birds. The major groups that are classified under this group are the Aves, Dromaeosaurus, Troodontids, Therizinosaurs and Oviraptors.

DROMAEOSAURIDE

This group of dinosaurs is more commonly called raptors. They were small to medium-sized feathered dinosaurs, appearing in the mid-Jurassic period. Some of the common examples of Dromaeosaurids are the Velociraptor and the Microraptor.

ABELISAURIDAE

This is a family of theropod dinosaurs that lived in Africa, South America and Asia during the Cretaceous period. Well-known examples of these dinosaurs are the Carnotaurus and the Abelisaurus.

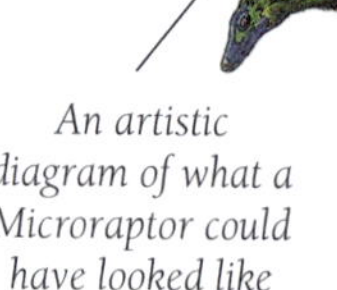

An artistic diagram of what a Microraptor could have looked like

Based on the few fossils recovered, experts believe this is what the Abelisaurus looked like

A 3D model showing what a Carnotaurus would have looked like

The Albertosaurus is a close relative of the Tyrannosaurus Rex

Possible interpretation of what a Tarbosaurus looked like

A possible representation of what the Gorgosaurus looked like

TYRANNOSAURIDAE

Tyrannosauridae are dinosaurs that belong to a family of bi-pedal meat eaters. This group of dinosaurs are known for their huge skulls, short arms and powerful jaws. Although they descended from smaller ancestors, tyrannosaurids were almost always the largest predators in their respective ecosystems, putting them at the top of the food chain. Perhaps the most famous dinosaur of all is the Tyrannosaurus Rex. Aside from this, other examples of the Tyrannosaurids are the Albertosaurus, Gorgosaurus and Tarbosaurus.

CARCHARODONTOSAURIDAE

Derived from the Greek word for 'shark-toothed lizards,' this is a family of dinosaurs that include some of the largest land carnivores that ever lived. Most of the Carcharodontosaurids had slender teeth, making it easy for them to grip and slice flesh when consuming their meals. Indentations in the arm have led some paleontologists to believe that some Carcharodontosaurids had quill-like feathers on their arm.The best examples of this family are the Gigantosaurus, Tyrannotitan, Carcharodontosaurus.

Due to its size, the Gigantosaurus often fed on juvenile sauropod dinosaurs.

What the Carcharodontosaurus might have looked like

At present, only three specimens of Tyrannotitan bones have been found by paleontologists

ALLOSAURIDAE

This is a family of dinosaurs who lived during the late Jurassic and early Cretaceous periods. The best known member of the family is the Allosaurus, a dinosaur who was at the top of the food chain during the late Jurassic period. Another example of Allosaurids is the Saurophaganax.

Although the Allosaurus preyed mostly on herbivorous dinosaurs, evidence indicates some of them resorted to cannibalism

A model showing what the Saurophaganx could have looked like

SPINOSAURIDAE

Spinosaurids were another family of large, bipedal, carnivorous dinosaurs. They had long, thin, crocodile-like skulls. There were some dinosaurs like the Spinosaurus and Baryonyx, that evolved into specialized fish-eaters. The Spinosaurus in particular had a large sail on its back. This sail was held up by spine-like bones, from which it got its famous name. In fact, the Spinosauridae family was named after the Spinosaurus, but it is worth noting that not all members of the family had a similar sail. Besides the two dinosaurs mentioned above, other examples of the Spinosauridae are the Suchomimus and the Irritator.

Possible interpretation of what a Suchomimus looked like

Representation of what a Baryonyx looked like.

With the help of modern technology, experts are able to construct a possible form of the Irritator, based on bones found during excavations.

The Spinosaurus was the biggest of all the carnivorous dinosaurs, living in the swamps of North Africa

SAUROPODS

Sauropods were a group of saurischian dinosaurs. They had very long necks, long tails, small heads (in relation to the rest of their body) and four thick legs. Sauropods are one of the most recognizable group of dinosaurs and have become a fixture in current culture thanks to their impressive size.They are notable for their enormous sizes and the group includes the largest animals to have ever lived on land. Sauropods first appeared in the late Triassic period. By the late Jurassic, the species had become widespread. The best-known examples of Sauropods include the Brachiosaurus, Diplodocus, Apatosaurus, Brontosaurus and Mamenchisaurus.

Initially used as an example of an ectothermic dinosaur, recent findings indicate that the Brachiosaurus was actually a warm-blooded animal.

Thanks to its large size, a fully-grown adult Diplodocus was too big to be preyed upon by any other dinosaur.

The Apatosaurus and other diplodocids could create loud noises if their tail was swung as fast as a whip.

The Brontosaurus is the most recognizable member of the Sauropod family. Thanks to this, the dinosaur has been featured in a variety of different mediums over the years.

TITANOSAURIA

Titanosauria were a diverse and the last surviving group of long-necked sauropods. The group's name is an allusion to the mythological Titans of Ancient Greece, thanks to how tall these dinosaurs were. They appeared around the early Cretaceous period and lived right up to the end of the Mesozoic era. Examples of these sauropods include Saltasaurus and Argentinosaurus.

A fully grown Argentinosaurus weighed nearly 100 tonnes

ORNITHISCHIANS

Ornithischians were a group of herbivorous dinosaurs, characterized by a pelvic structure similar to birds. Ornithischians with well-known anatomical adaptations include the horn-faced dinosaurs (like the Triceratops), armored dinosaurs (like the stegosaurs and ankylosaurs, Pachycephalosaurids and ornithopods). Evidence found from different excavation sites indicate that certain groups of ornithischians lived in herds and were segregated based on age group, with the young forming their own flocks, separate from adults. There were some specimens which were partially covered in filamentous hair or feather-like pelts and has since been the subject of an on-going debate.

An interesting feature of Ornithischians is how they all shared a unique bone called the predentary. This bone was located at the front of the lower jaw and coincided with the premaxilla in the upper jaw. This formed a beak-like apparatus that was used to clip off plant material. Interestingly enough, the Chilesaurus represents an early ornithischian that had not yet evolved a predentary seen in later specimens. Some of the best-known types of Ornithischian dinosaurs are listed below.

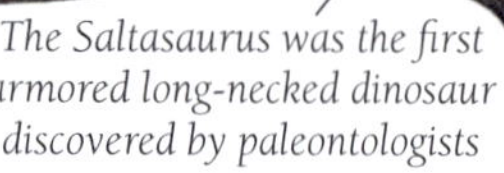

The Saltasaurus was the first armored long-necked dinosaur discovered by paleontologists

A drawing of a Triceratops skull. Note the Predentary bone located on the lower jaw

A model of what the Hesperosaurus could have looked like.

Drawing showing what a Wuerhosaurus might have looked like.

A model of the Kentrosaurus

The plates on the back of the Stegosaurus is thought to have been used as a form of display and for thermoregulatory functions

THYREOPHORA

Thyreophora was a branch from the ornithischian group. It literally translates to 'shield bearers.' However, they are often called by another name 'armored dinosaurs.' Thyreophorans were heavily armored dinosaurs with thick skin and rows of plates that spanned the length of their bodies. There were some dinosaurs which took their protection a step further by evolving spikes or tail clubs. The two best known groups of Thyreophorans were Ankylosauria and Stegosauria.

STEGOSAURIA

Cycads are seed plants that have existed for many centuries and were once more common than what is seen today.

Stegosauria were a group of herbivorous dinosaurs that lived between the Jurassic and early Cretaceous periods. After an early evolutionary innovation involving tail spikes as defensive weapons, the dinosaurs became larger and developed long hindlimbs that no longer allowed them to run. This increased the importance of the tail spikes, which could potentially ward off large predators. Their necks grew longer and their small heads became narrow, allowing them to bite only the best parts of Cycads with their beaks. When these plants began to decline in diversity, so too did the Stegosauria, which became extinct by the first half of the Cretaceous period. Some of the examples of Stegosauria are Hesperosaurus, Wuerhosaurus, Kentrosaurus and Stegosaurus.

ANKYLOSAURIA

Ankylosauria were a group of herbivorous dinosaurs with armor on their body, in the form of bony osteoderms. Ankylosaurs were bulky quadrupeds with short yet powerful limbs. They first appeared in the early Jurassic period and persisted till the end of the Cretaceous period. The remains of these dinosaurs have been found on every continent, with the first being discovered in Antarctica in 1986.

Ankylosauria had armor covering much of their bodies. This armor was rectangular or oval in shape. The skull also had armor plastered onto it, including a distinctive piece on the outside-rear of the lower jaw. There were even some which developed tail clubs that were used as a deterrent against predators. Examples of ankylosauria are Minmi, Edmontonia, Polacanthus and Ankylosaurus.

A possible illustration of the Minmi, based on fragmentary remains found by paleontologists

Many paleontologists believe that the spikes on the side of the body were used by male Edmontonia in contests of strength

Model of a Polacanthus

HADROSAURIDAE

More commonly known as duck-billed dinosaurs, the Hadrosauridae owe their name to the flat duck-bill like appearance of bones in their snouts. This was a common group of herbivorous dinosaurs present during the late Cretaceous period. They are a family of dinosaurs that descended from Iguanodontian dinosaurs and had a similar body layout. Hadrosaurids were facultative bipeds, i.e., they walked on two legs when young, and walked on four legs when they grew older. Some examples of Hadrosaurids are the Lambeosaurus, Edmontosaurus, Parasaurolophus and Hadrosaurus.

Although there is no definitive conclusion on what the cranial crest of the Lambeosaurus was used for, many experts have suggested it had a wide array of uses from improving the sense of smell, being a resonating chamber for making sounds or had some importance among the social hierarchy.

Thanks to the abundance of fossils recovered, researchers have learned that the Edmontosaurus lived in groups and often migrated.

Due to only a handful of good specimens excavated, experts find it difficult to ascertain the function of the Parasaurolophus' crest.

A model of the Hadrosaurus based on skeletal mounts and fossil diagrams.

PACHYCEPHALOSAURIA

It was a type of dinosaur which lived during the late Cretaceous period. These dinosaurs were bipedal and had thick skulls (which is why their name translates to 'thick headed lizards'). Many members of this group had domed skulls and these often had spikes. Experts believe that Pachycephalosaurians fought each other by ramming their heads - similar to how stags fight today in order to establish dominance. Examples of this type are the Stegoceras and Pachycephalosaurus.

Many experts believe that Pachycephalosaurus lived on a diet of leaves, seeds and fruits.

CERATOPSIA

Ceratopsia was a group of dinosaurs known for having horns on their faces. Their ancestors first emerged during the Jurassic period and their descendants became common in the Cretaceous period. Like other Ornithischians, Ceratopsia were herbivorous. They had beak-like mouth parts, elaborate facial horns extending over the neck, with the most famous of them being the Triceratops. While these frills were used to protect their neck from predators, the frills are also thought to have been used for display and thermoregulation.

Other dinosaurs of this group include the Centrosaurus and the Psittacosaurus.

Stegoceras were herbivorous dinosaurs with a good sense of smell.

Construction of a Centrosaurus based on evidence collected from various sites.

There is an ongoing debate among paleontologists as to what is the purpose of the long quills found on the dinosaur's tail.

Of the three horns on the triceratops, the third horn on the snout was not as powerful as the other two.

Evolutionary origins

The first known dinosaurs were bipedal predators, which were 1-2 metres long. Early confirmed dinosaur fossils include Saurischian dinosaurs like the Nyasasaurus, Saturnalia, Herrerasaurus, Stayrikosaurus, Eoraptor and Alwalkeria. The earliest ornithischian dinosaur found was the Pisanosaurus. Early Saurischians did resemble early ornithischians. Saurischians were noticeably different from ornithischians except for the ancestral bone configuration in the pelvis. Another difference between the two types is seen in the skull. The upper skull of Ornithischians is more solid and the joint that links the lower jaw is more flexible, both of which can be seen in the Lesothosaurus.

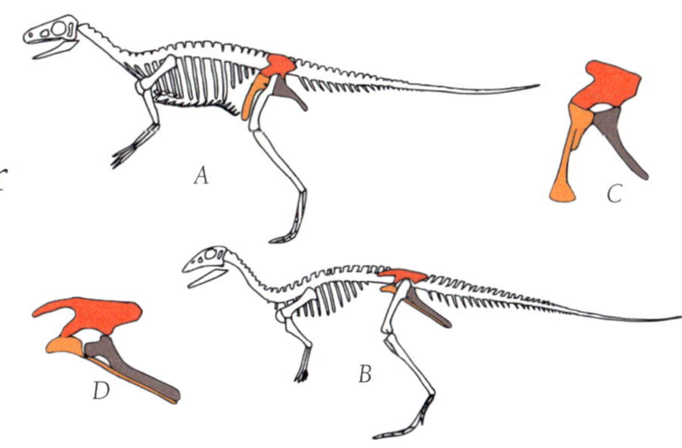

A. Eoraptor, an early Saurischian, B. Lesothosaurus, a primitive ornithischian, C. Pelvis of a Staurikosaurus, D. Pelvis of a Lesothosaurus

FOSSIL RECORDS

The first few lines of primitive dinosaurs diversified rapidly through the Triassic period. Dinosaur species quickly evolved the special features and range of sizes needed to exploit every terrestrial ecological niche. In this period of dinosaur predominance spanning the length of the Jurassic and Cretaceous periods, nearly every known land animal larger than 1 metre in length was a dinosaur.

A chart showing the size of various Theropods in comparison to a human

One measure of the quality of the fossil record is done by comparing the date of first appearance with the order of branching of a cladogram based on the shape of fossil elements. Most dinosaur fossils were found in the Triassic, Jurassic and Cretaceous periods.

EVOLUTION IN BODY SIZE

Body size is an important feature in evolution as it correlates to metabolism, diet, life history, geographic range and extinction rate. The modal body mass of dinosaurs was somewhere between 1- 10 tonnes through the Mesozoic era across all major continental regions. There was a trend towards increasing body size with many dinosaur groups, including the Thyreophora, Ornithopoda, Pachycephalosauria, Certaopsia, Sauropomorpha and Theropods. There is a noticeable decrease in body size that has occurred in some lineages of dinosaurs, but these instances are very sporadic. In fact, the best known example of a decrease in body size is the one leading up to the first birds. A creature like the Archaeopteryx was less than ten kilograms and later birds like the Sinomis and Confuciusornis weighed about as much as a starling or a pigeon. This occured with the intent of easier flight.

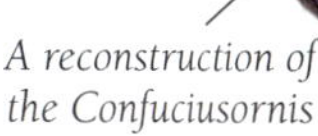

A reconstruction of the Confuciusornis

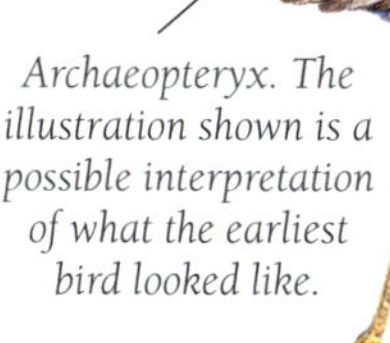

Archaeopteryx. The illustration shown is a possible interpretation of what the earliest bird looked like.

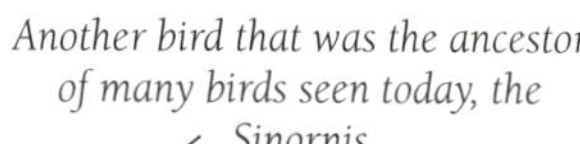

Another bird that was the ancestor of many birds seen today, the Sinornis

EVOLUTION IN MOBILITY

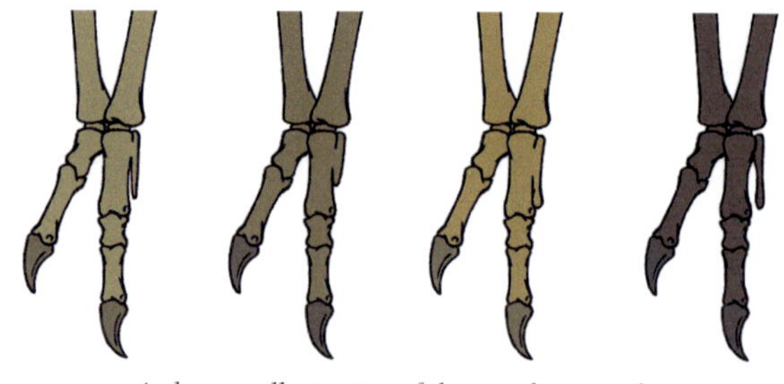

A close up illustration of the two digits on the forelimbs of tyrannosaurids.

The ancestral dinosaur was a biped. Later, evolution into a quadrupedal posture happened four times among the ancestors of Euornithopoda, Thyreophora, Ceratopsia and Sauropodomorpha. In the cases of these four dinosaurs, the evolution in mobility was associated with an increase in body size and the change could not be reversed, i.e., it was unidirectional. Dinosaurs show a pattern of reduction and loss of fingers on the lateral side. The purpose of a dinosaurs hand was to grasp an object with a partly opposable thumb. The reduction of digits is one of the defining features of tyrannosaurids, only having two digits on very short forelimbs.

Illustration showing how early Ceratopsia were biped dinosaurs but as they slowly evolved, they became quadruped.

EVOLUTIONARY EFFECTS ON FOOD SOURCES

Most dinosaurs were carnivorous in nature. There were some herbivores seen in the ornithischian, sauropodomorph and therizinosaurid groups. As this happened, it is speculated that plants also evolved in accordance with herbivorous dinosaurs emerging. The appearance of prosauropods in the late Triassic period has been linked either to the demise or diversification of types of flora at that time. The rise of ceratopsids and hadrosaurid ornithopods in the Cretaceous period has been liked to angiosperm radiation. While these theories do show a correlation to plants evolving alongside dinosaurs, no hard evidence can be found. In fact, paleontologists only know about the chewing techniques of herbivorous dinosaurs and have little to no data on their dietary preferences.

Parasaurolophus

Maissaurus

PALEOGEOGRAPHY

During the early Cretaceous period and the ongoing breakup of Pangea, dinosaurs were becoming strongly differentiated by landmass. The earliest part of the time saw the spread of Ankylosaurians, Iguanodontians and Brachiosaurids through Europe, North America and northern Africa. These were later supplemented or replaced in Africa by Spinosaurid and Carcharodontosaurid theropods. In Asia, groups like dromaeosaurids, troodontids and oviraptorosaurians became common while Ankylosaurids and early Ceratopsians became important herbivores to the ecology. Australia was home to Ankylosaurians, Hypsilophodonts and Iguanodontians. A major change in the early Cretaceous period that further developed during the late Cretaceous period was the evolution of flowering plants. At the same time, many herbivorous dinosaurs evolved more sophisticated ways to orally process their food. Ceratopsians had a method of slicing their food, with the teeth stacked on each other in batteries and Iguanadontians refined a method of grinding with tooth batteries. Some Sauropods also evolved tooth batteries, the most well-known being the Nigersaurus.

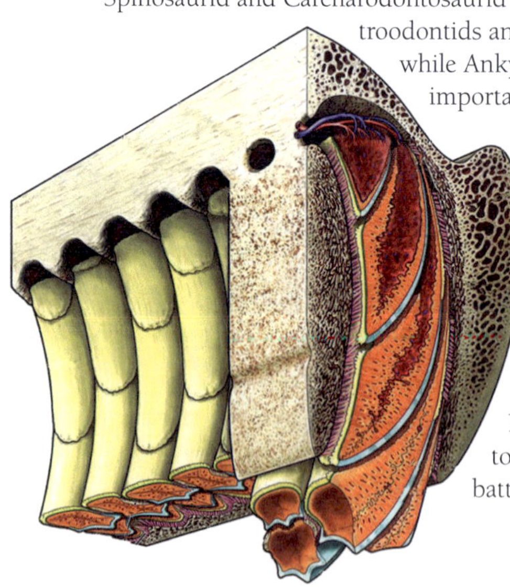

Illustration of a tooth battery. The upper and lower batteries ground against each other when the herbivorous dinosaur chewed it's food and this system allowed these dinosaurs to chew their food efficiently.

Ultrsaurus

Styracosaurus

Saltasaurus

Ankylosaurids

QUICK FACTS

The hadrosaurids had what scientists call a "dental battery," meaning they had hundreds of teeth that worked together when they ate, with new teeth "erupting" into the mouth all the time.

SPREAD OF DINOSAURS

There were three general dinosaur faunas in the late Cretaceous period. In places like North America and Asia, the major theropods were tyrannosaurids and differed kinds of maniraptoran theropods, with a predominantly ornithischian herbivore assembly. In the southern continents, abelisaurds were the common theropods and titanosaurian sauropods were the common herbivores. Lastly in Europe, dromaeosaurids, rhabdodontid iguanodontians, nodosaurid ankylosaurians, and titanosaurian sauropods ruled the area. Flowering plants were normally radiating, with the first grasses appearing by the end of the Cretaceous period. Grinding Hadrosaurids and shearing Ceratopsians became extremely diverse across North America and Asia. Theropods were also radiating as herbivores or omnivores with therizinosaurians and ornthomimosaurians becoming common.

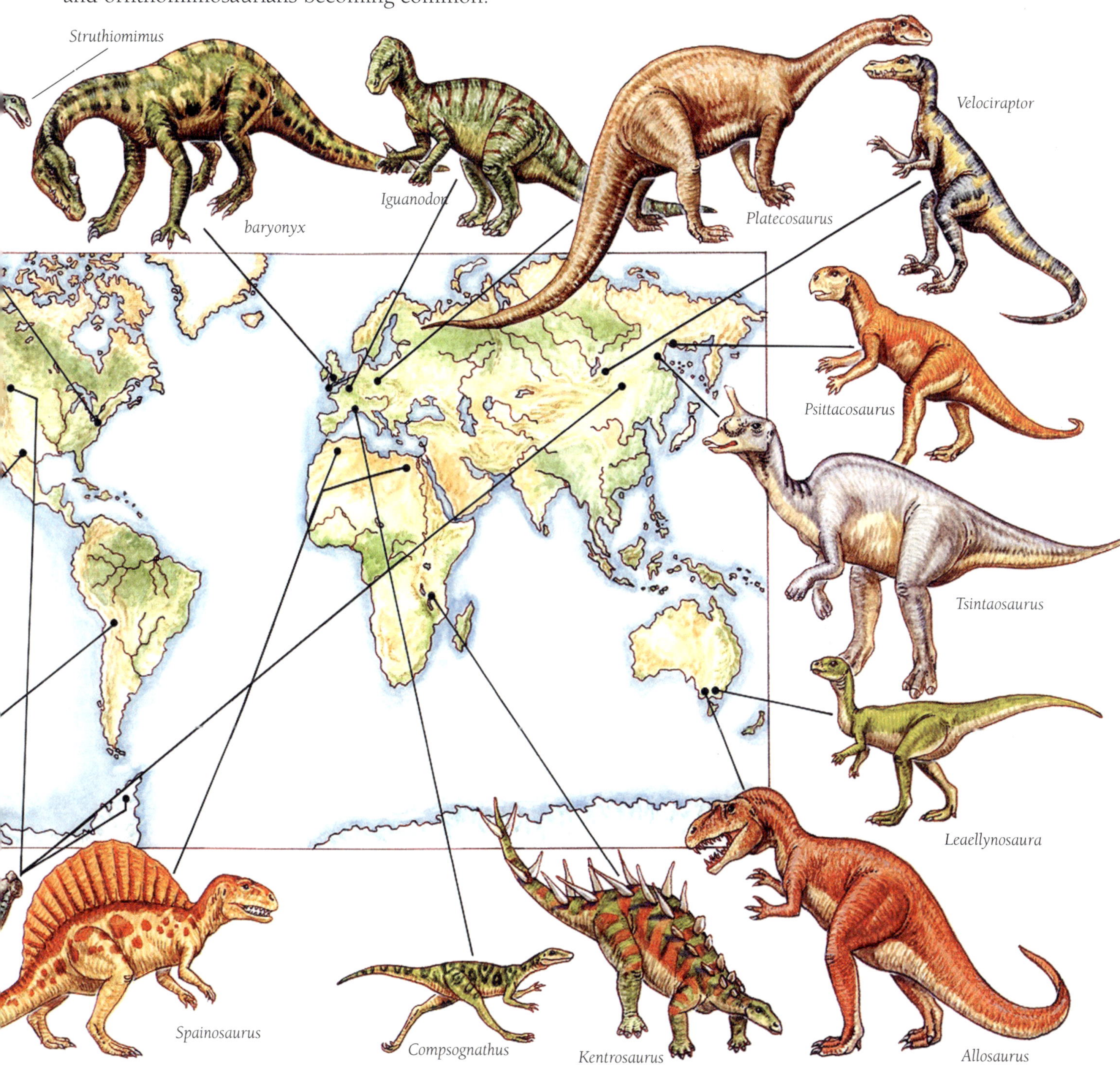

Diagram providing a general idea about the distribution of dinosaurs during the Cretaceous period.

Arrangement according to size

Size has been one of the more interesting aspects of dinosaur science for both scientists and the public. Dinosaurs show some of the most extreme variations in size of any land animal group, the size ranging from hummingbirds to Titanosaurs. While scientists for many years have gathered information and constructed various models from the evidence available, experts can never be certain of the largest and smallest dinosaurs to have ever existed. This is because only a tiny fraction of animals ever fossilizes and most fossils remain buried in the earth. Of this small percentage, the few that are recovered are complete skeletons and impressions of skin or other soft tissues are not exactly a dime a dozen. Therefore, rebuilding a complete skeleton by comparing the size and morphology of bones to those of similar, better-known species is an inexact art and rebuilding the muscles or organs of the animal is at best, a process of educated guesswork.

Theropod dinosaur

This process affects the weight estimate for dinosaurs. Though advances in technology allow experts to laser scan the skeleton and put a 'virtual' skin over it, the process is still an estimate and not a completely accurate reading. Current evidence suggests that the average size of a dinosaur varied through the Triassic period, the Jurassic period and the Cretaceous periods.

Sauropods were the largest and heaviest dinosaurs. For much of the dinosaur era, the smallest sauropods were larger than anything else in their habitat. Giant mammals like the Paraceratherium and Palaeoloxodon were dwarfed by sauropods and only modern whales could surpass them in size. One of the tallest and heaviest dinosaurs known from good skeletal remains is the Giraffatitan Brancai. One of the longest complete dinosaurs is the Diplodocus.

A scale diagram which compares a human against the largest known dinosaurs of the five major categories.

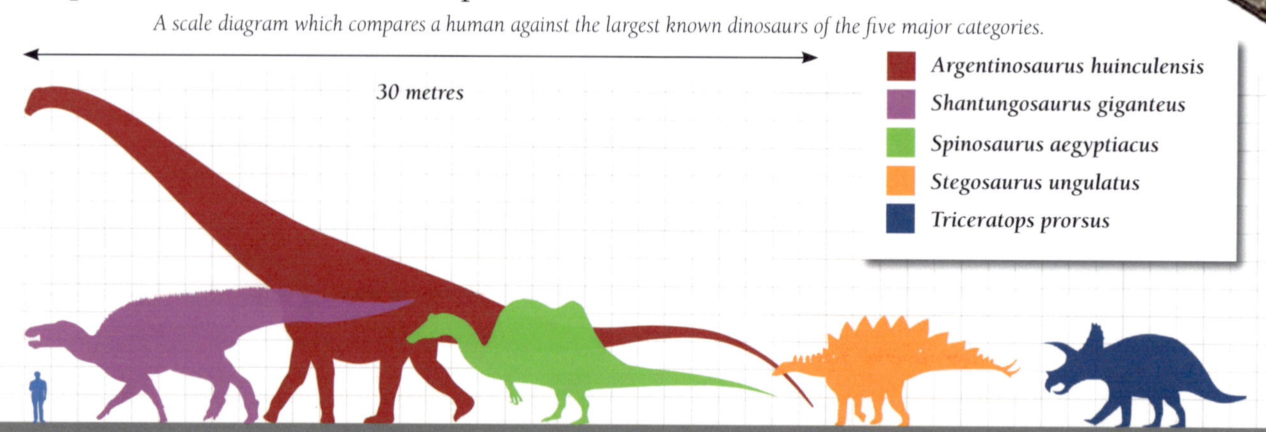

FROM LARGE TO SMALL

There were larger dinosaurs, but knowledge of them is based on a few fragmentary fossils found over the years. The Titanosaur was the largest dinosaur known from uncontroversial evidence, estimated to have been 30-39.7 metres long.

For many decades, the Tyrannosaurus was the largest theropod and best-known dinosaur according to the general public. Since its discovery, however, a number of other giant carnivorous dinosaurs have been described. This includes the Spinosaurus, the Gigantosaurus and the Carcharodontosaurus. These large theropod dinosaurs rivaled or even surpassed the Tyrannosaurus in size but not in weight.

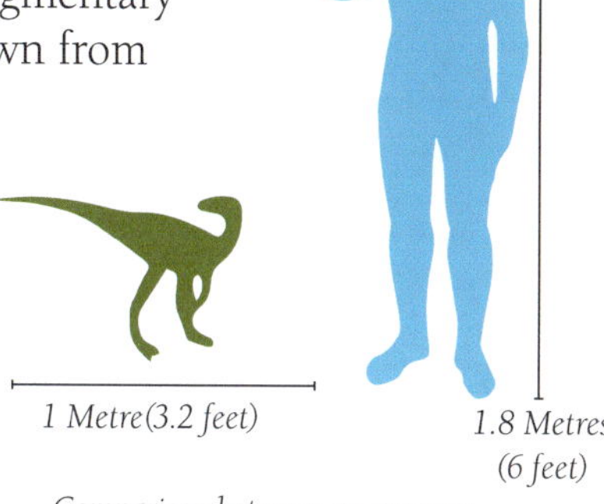

Comparison between an average human and an Eoraptor

Recent theories propose that the theropod body size shrank over the past 50 million years from an average of 163 kilograms to 0.8 kilograms, as they eventually evolved into modern birds. This theory is based on evidence that Theropods were the only dinosaurs to get smaller and their skeletons changed four times faster as opposed to the other dinosaur species. The illustrations below show the lengths of different dinosaurs compared to an average human.

Length of the smallest Theropods when compared to a human.

Longest Theropods in comparison to a human.

Illustration showing the length of Giant Ornithopods against an average human

Illustration of average Ceratopsians against man

The length and height of Pachycephalosaurus in comparison to an average human

Comparison between a normal human and Stegoasurus

Titanosaurus

Length of an average Ankylosaurus

Behaviour of dinosaurs

Many birds are highly social, often found living in large groups. This had led to a general agreement where some behaviours that are common in birds are also seen in crocodiles and were thus common among extinct dinosaur groups. Interpretations of their behaviour in fossil species are generally based on the pose of skeletons and their habitat, computer simulations of their biomechanics and comparisons with modern animals in similar ecological niches.

The first potential evidence for herding or flocking as a widespread behaviour common to many dinosaur groups came in 1878, with the discovery of 31 Iguanodon Bernissartensis, a group that at first were thought to have perished in Belgium, after they fell into a sinkhole and drowned. Other mass-death sites have later been discovered.

This evidence, coupled with multiple trackways, suggests that such behaviour was common among many early dinosaur species. Trackways of hundreds or thousands of herbivores indicate that Hadrosaurids must have moved together in great herds (a trend common among the American bison or the African Springbok). Sauropod tracks document that these animals travelled in groups made up of several different species, at least in Oxfordshire, England, despite there being no evidence for specific herd structures, making all these theories speculative at best.

A herd of different dinosaurs roaming pre-historic England.

PACK MENTALITY

Congregating into herds may have come about as a defensive measure, for migratory purposes or to provide protection for the young. There is evidence that many types of slow-moving dinosaurs like theropods, sauropods, ankylosaurians, ornithopods and ceratopsians formed groups for a variety of reasons. One example of this is a site found in Inner Mongolia which contains the remains of more than 20 Sinornithomimus, from one to seven years old. This assembly is seen as a social group that was trapped in mud and died as a result.

There is also the common belief which depicted carnivorous theropods acting as pack hunters and working together in order to take down large prey. However, this type of behaviour is not seen in descendants like birds, crocodiles and other reptiles. Furthermore, taphonomic evidence suggests how mammal-like pack hunting theropods like the Allosaurus and Deinoychus can also be seen as the results of fatal disputes between feeding animals, as is seen in many of the dinosaur's descendants.

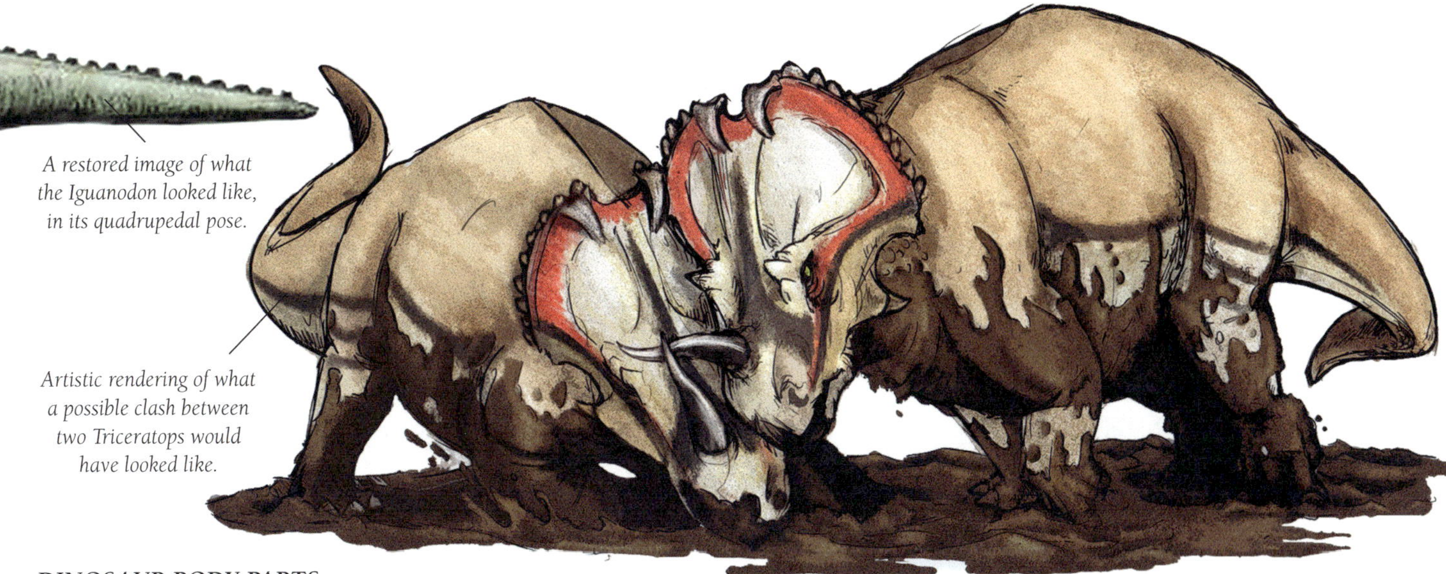

A restored image of what the Iguanodon looked like, in its quadrupedal pose.

Artistic rendering of what a possible clash between two Triceratops would have looked like.

DINOSAUR BODY PARTS

The crests and frills of some dinosaurs like the marginocephalians, lambeosaurines and theropods might be too frail to be used for active defense. This is why scientists believe they were likely used for displays of power or for establishing dominance. Head wounds from bites also suggest that theropods, did at least engage in active aggressive confrontations. However, experts have little knowledge about dinosaur mating habits and territorialism, so many suggestions are just that, suggestive. Due to there being no definitive proof of what these frills were used for, there is no way of knowing which suggestions are correct and which are wrong.

From a behavioural perspective, one of the most valuable dinosaur fossils was found in the Gobi Desert in 1971. The fossil was a Velociraptor attacking a Protoceratops, providing evidence that dinosaurs did indeed attack each other. Additional evidence was later found showing a partially healed tail of an Edmontosaurus. The tail was bitten off by a tyrannosaur but the dinosaur survived the attack. Experts also believe that cannibalism was common among some species of dinosaurs, evidenced by tooth marks found in Madagascar in 2003, involving a theropod Majungasaurus.

MORE STONES TO TURN

A good understanding of how dinosaurs moved on the ground is important to learn more about dinosaur behaviour. The science of biomechanics has provided a great deal of insight in this area. For example, studies of the forces exerted by muscles and gravity on dinosaurs' skeletal structure have shown how fast dinosaurs could run, whether diplodocids could create a sonic boom when whipping their tails and whether sauropods could float.

In informal usage, the Dromaeosaurids are often called raptors.

Originally, the dinosaur was called Syntarsus, but the name was already taken by a beetle hence the name changing to Megapnosaurus.

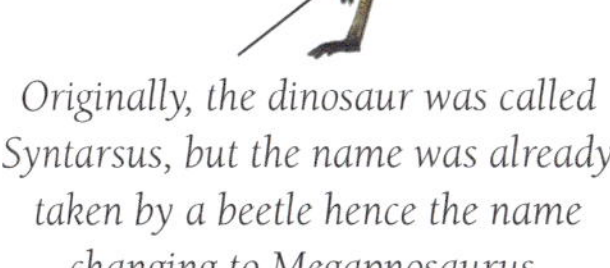

The average length of a Juravenator is 75 cm long.

A tenontosaurus set upon by a pack of theropod carnivores.'

EVEN DINOSAURS SLEPT

Comparisons between the scleral rings of dinosaurs to modern birds and reptiles have shed some light into the daily activity pattern of dinosaurs. Although it is suggested that most dinosaurs were active during the day, some comparisons have shown how small predatory dinosaurs like Dromaeosaurids, Juravenator and Megapnosaurus were most likely nocturnal. Large and medium-sized dinosaurs like the ceratopsians, sauropodomorphs, hadrosaurids and ornithomimosaurs may have been cathemeral i.e., active during short intervals throughout the day, while ornithischian like Agilisaurus was thought to be diurnal i.e., active during the day and slept at night.

How they were born?

Dinosaurs eggs are the organic vessels in which a dinosaur embryo forms and develops. When the first scientifically documented remains of dinosaurs were being described in England in the 1820's, it was already presumed that dinosaurs did lay eggs because they were ancestors to reptiles. In 1859, the first scientifically documented dinosaur egg fossils were discovered in France by Catholic priest Jean-Jacques Poech, although he famously mistook them for giant bird eggs. The first scientifically recognized dinosaur egg fossils were discovered in 1923 in Mongolia by a crew from the American Museum of Natural History. Since then, many new nesting sites have been found all over the world and a system of classification based on the structure of the eggshell was created. This system was first conceptualized in China before moving to the west.

DINOSAURS AND NESTS

All dinosaurs laid amniotic eggs with shells composed of calcium carbonate. These eggs were laid in a nest. There were many dinosaurs who often made elaborate nests which could be cups, domes, plates, bed scrapes, mounds or burrows. There are some species of modern birds who don't even make nests. The male emperor penguins for example keep the eggs between their feet and the guillemot lays its eggs on bare rock.

A Guillemot egg laid on the rock. The nests of the Guillemot are laid in densely packed colonies known as loomeries.

Primitive birds and many non-avian dinosaurs often laid their eggs in communal nests and the males took part in incubating these eggs till maturation. Although modern birds have a single oviduct and thus lay eggs one at a time, pre-historic birds had two oviducts, like crocodiles. Also, there were some non-avian dinosaurs like the Troodon which exhibited iterative laying, where the adult may lay a pair of eggs every one or two days, then ensured simultaneous hatching by delaying brooding till all eggs were laid.

FINDING THESE NESTS

The first signs of fossilized dinosaur eggs awaiting discovery are finding shell fragments eroded away from the original eggs and transported down by the elements. From this, paleontologists begin searching for the nest area. After this, they estimate the arrangement of eggs. Excavation proceeds to significant depth as many dinosaur nests had multiple layers of eggs. After extracting the fossils, the eggs are then cleaned in a laboratory, requiring a great deal of patience and skill.

Possibly how the Troodon could have looked like.

ADDITIONAL GROWTH

During the process of reproduction, females grow a special type of bone between the hard, outer bone and the marrow of their limbs. This medullary bone, rich in calcium is used to make eggshells. During an examination of a Tyrannosaurus Rex skeleton, paleontologists had found evidence of a medullary bone in the dinosaurs and, for the first time, this allowed experts to properly establish the sex of a fossil dinosaur specimen. Additional research found the same medullary bone in the carnosaur Allosaurus and the ornithopod Tenotosaurus.

It has been understood that the line of dinosaurs that included the Allosaurus and Tyrannosaurus diverged from the line that led to Tenotosaurus was very early in the evolution of dinosaurs. This has led to the belief that the production of the medullary tissue was a general characteristic of all dinosaurs.

Cross section of a T-Rex, with the medullary bone, an indication that the dinosaur was pregnant at the time.

PARENTAL CARE

Isle of Skye is often called Scotland's Dinosaur Isle due to the many well-preserved dinosaur footprints on the island.

Another widespread trait among modern birds is the parental care exhibited to the children after hatching from the egg. According to a 1978 discovery of a Maiasaura nesting ground in Montana, United States, evidence clearly indicated that parental care continued long after birth in the ornithopods. A specimen of Mongolian oviraptorid dinosaurs were discovered in a chicken-like brooding position in 1993, which could possibly indicate the dinosaurs may have started using an insulating layer of feathers as a way to keep the eggs warm.

Another dinosaur embryo indicated the absence of teeth. This led to the theory that some parental care was required to feed the young dinosaurs for a set period of time. In the Isle of Skye in northwestern Scotland, evidence in the form of trackways also confirms parental behaviour among ornithopods.

The true story of birds

Perhaps the most interesting questions in paleontology and evolution is the origin of birds. The discovery that birds came from dinosaurs during the late Jurassic period was made possible only through the recently discovered fossils from China, South America and other countries. Additionally, looking at old museum specimens from new perspectives and new methods also supported the cause. The hunt for the ancestors of living birds started with a specimen of the Archaeopteryx, the first known bird, discovered in the early 1860's.

THOMAS, THE ANATOMIST

Thomas Henry Huxley, a comparative anatomist made a study of this nearly 150 years ago. In it, he compared a fossil of the Archaeopteryx to a small theropod, Compsognathus. Their fossils were found in the Solnhofen limestone in Bavaria Germany and dated back to 144 million years ago.

Huxley's study revealed that the two fossils were almost identical, save for the front limbs and feathers of the Archaeopteryx. Thanks to this, he united the classes of reptiles and birds under Sauropsida and believed that birds originally came from small theropod dinosaurs.

Although Huxley's idea was a revolutionary one, it took a long time before his peers and other paleontologists came around to it. It was the discovery of feathered dinosaurs and birds in the Lower Cretaceous of China that finally convinced them. From what they understood, theropod dinosaurs evolved feathers not as a means of flight, but instead for heat regulation. From that point on, a small group of theropods started using them for primitive flight. This group is represented on the evolutionary ladder by the Archaeopteryx and Anchiomis.

Huxley had pointed out that Archaeopteryx was a mixture of reptile and bird features. Without the feathers and arms, the skeleton looked like that of the Compsognathus. Based on its bone growth, physiology was much slower than modern birds and was comparatively similar to Archaeopteryx's dinosaur ancestors. This means it would take longer after hatching to learn how to fly. A modern bird takes 3-6 weeks from hatching to flying. When compared to the Archaeopteryx, scientists believe it took 18 weeks to perform the same feat. This in turn is an example of mosaic evolution, where some characters in a transitional form are primitive while later forms are remarkably advanced.

Due to his strong and tenacious support of the Archaeopteryx being a transitional fossil between birds and reptiles, and his support of Darwin's theory of evolution, Thomas Huxley was often called 'Darwin's Bulldog.'

A number of anatomical features are shared by both birds and theropod dinosaurs.

FEATHERS

One of the many possible versions of what the Archaeopteryx could have looked like.

Anchiornishuxlei, the only dinobird fossil that lived before Archaeopteryx was found in Liaoning, China. It had large wings, with light feathers attached to the arm and feathers on the hind legs, forming an arrangement of fore and hind wings. The forewing had 11 primary and 10 secondary feathers. Further studies indicate the primary feathers indicated poorer aerodynamic ability when compared to its later relatives. Based on the design and arrangement of feathers, Anchironishuxlei could glide but not fly.

The Archaeopteryx fossil found in Germany was a transitional fossil, with features clearly intermediate between those of non-avian theropod dinosaurs and birds. Since the 1990's, a number of other feathered dinosaurs have been found, further providing evidence of the relationship between dinosaurs and modern birds. These specimens were unearthed in China, which was part of an island continent during the Cretaceous Period. Though feathers have been found in only a few locations, it is still possible that some non-avian dinosaurs in other parts of the world also had feathers. However, the lack of widespread fossil evidence for non-avian dinosaurs may be a result of features like skin and feathers rarely being preserved by fossilization.

Direct fossil evidence of feathers or feather-like structures have been found in a diverse array of species in many non-avian dinosaur groups. Evidence for true, vaned feather, similar to the ones used by modern birds have been found in the theropod subgroup Maniraptora, which includes oviraptorosaurs, troodontids and dromaeosaurids. Feather-like structures called pycnofibres have been found in pterosaurs, leading to the possibility that feather-like filaments may have been common in birds and have evolved from dinosaurs themselves.

Thanks to advancements in technology, pigments preserved in a 120-million-year-old fossil bird was revealed during X-rays. Paleontologists were able to scan the fossils before publishing their findings in a reputed source. Their studies reveal the chemical fingerprint of pigments that once tinted these ancient bird's feathers. The trace metal copper is a marker for the dark pigment eumelanin. The X-ray technique used by the paleontologists was accurate enough, it showed that each copper molecule was tugged and squashed into a particular shape before being bound within a eumelanin molecule.

QUICK FACTS

Since its discovery, Pterosaur, like the Tyrannosaurus Rex, has become very popular in movies and T.V shows.

Archaeopteryx fossil found in Bavaria, Germany

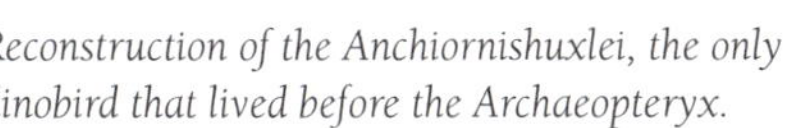

Reconstruction of the Anchiornishuxlei, the only dinobird that lived before the Archaeopteryx.

USAGE OF FEATHERS BY DINOSAURS

The functions of feathers have long been debated among scientists. The first type of feathers, which were simple and hair-like in design were used for insulation. But for later theropods, such as some oviraptors, the feathers on the arms and hands were long, despite the forelimbs themselves being short. This begs the question, what did dinosaurs do with these long feathers on short arms? One suggestion comes from a well-preserved fossil in the Gobi Desert. This fossil of oviraptorosaurs dating back to the Cretaceous period shows the dinosaur hunched up on a nest of eggs, similar to a brooding chicken. This leads to the theory that the feathers were used to warm the eggs and perhaps shield them from predators.

Reconstruction of how the oviraptorosaur possibly protected its eggs.

As dinosaurs with feathers slowly evolved, allowing some to fly, these early birds had access to new habitats resulting in rapid evolution. Evidence of this is seen in the Chinese fossils, which are more varied and more advanced than the Archaeopteryx. Studies also indicate how some of these birds used feathers for signaling and display, a trait common among birds today.

Birds were among the few survivors to come out of the dinosaur extinction, lending to the theory that birds were not just descendants of reptiles, but also the descendant of theropod dinosaurs. This meant that birds are the last surviving dinosaurs.

SKELETON

As a result of how feathers are a vital part of birds, feathered dinosaurs are often seen as the missing link between dinosaurs and birds. However, the multiple skeletal features also shared by the two groups represent another important line of evidence, the skeleton. Areas of the skeleton that have important similarities include the neck, pubis, a part of the wrist, arm, pectoral girdle, wishbone and breast bone. By comparing the skeletons of both birds and dinosaurs through cladistic analysis, the case of feathered dinosaurs being the missing link is only further strengthened.

A study comparing embryonic, juvenile and adult archosaur skulls concludes that bird skulls are derived from those of theropod dinosaurs by progenesis, a type of paedomorphic heterochrony, which resulted in retention of the juvenile characteristics of their ancestors.

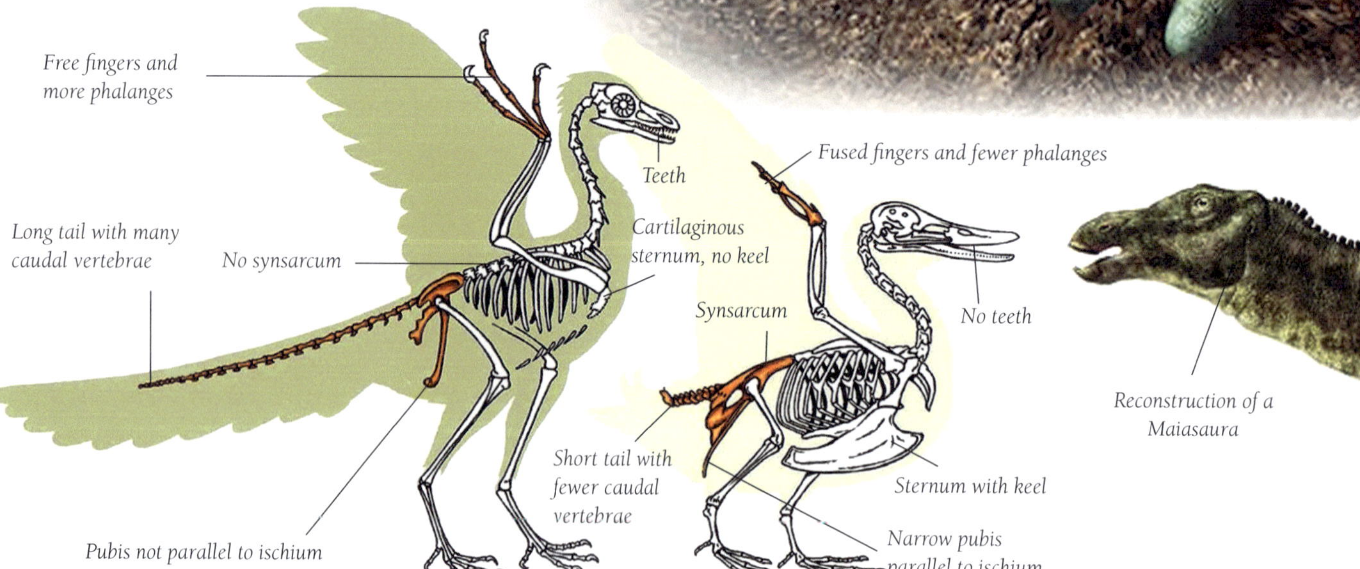

Reconstruction of a Maiasaura

Skeleton of an Archaeopteryx, showing how similar dinosaur skeletons from years ago resemble birds.

SOFT ANATOMY

According to a study published in 2005, large meat-eating dinosaurs had a complex system of air sacs, similar to those found in modern birds. The lungs of theropod dinosaurs likely pumped air into hollow sacs in their skeletons, which is also another feature similar to birds. In 2008, scientists performed a CT scan on an Aerosteonriocoloradensis, revealing evidence for the existence of air sacs inside the body. This finding was the strongest evidence of a dinosaur having a bird-like breathing system.

SLEEPING POSTURE

Fossils of the Troodonts Mei and Sinornithoides show that dinosaurs slept like modern birds, with their heads tucked under their arms. This behavior helped them in keeping their head warm and, is also another characteristic shared with birds.

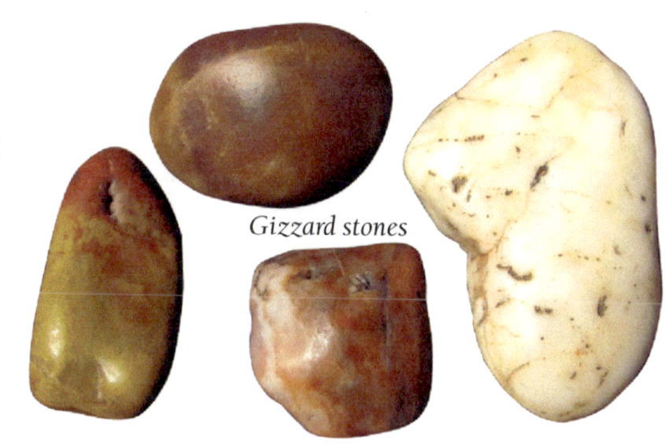

Gizzard stones

GIZZARD STONES

Both birds and dinosaurs use gizzard stones. These stones were swallowed to aid in digestion and break down hard fibers once they enter the stomach. Gizzard stones, when found in association with fossils are called gastroliths.

Aside from this, there have been several occasions where the extraction of DNA and proteins from Mesozoic dinosaur fossils has been claimed, allowing for a comparison with birds. Several proteins have been detected in dinosaur fossils, one of which being haemoglobin.

QUICK FACTS

Precocial refers to species in which the young ones are mature and mobile from the moment they are born or hatched.

BROODING AND CARE OF YOUNG

There have been a number of fossils recovered, showing them resting over the eggs in a nest in a position similar to brooding. A number of dinosaur species like the Maiasaura have been found in herds of young and adult individuals, suggesting a degree of interaction between them. The ratio between egg volume and body mass of adults suggests these eggs were brooded by the male and that the young were highly precocial, a trait seen in many birds after hatching.

There was also a dinosaur embryo found without teeth, suggesting the adult dinosaur might have regurgitated the food into the young dinosaur's mouth, feeding the young dinosaur in the process. This behaviour is seen in almost every species of bird on the planet.

Aquatic dinosaurs

Through the years, some dinosaurs took to the water, adapting to the new environment and becoming the first air breathing hunters in the oceans. These were aquatic reptiles and many of them evolved to dominate their food chain. The two most dominant dinosaurs of the sea were the Ichthyosaur and Plesiosaur, while there were other dangerous reptiles like the Dakosaurus, Archelon, Mosasaurs and Pachyrhachis.

3D reconstruction of what a Dakosaur could have looked like.

Fossil of a Pachyrhachis, an ancient marine snake which had a hip, knee and ankle joint.

Picture of an Archelon in comparison to an average human.

Reconstruction of a mosasaur.

ICHTHYOSAUR

Ichthyosaurs were giant marine reptiles which were visually similar to fish and dolphins but had long snouts like crocodiles. They lived during much of the Mesozoic era and were one of the dominant reptiles in the sea while dinosaurs ruled the land.

A consensus among experts states that Ichthyosaurs are animals descended from terrestrial egg-laying dinosaurs during the late Premian period or the early Triassic period. Experts however, had trouble on placing the ichthyosaur on the amniote evolutionary tree.

Computer Graphics reconstruction of an Ichthyosaur.

HOW THEY MOVED

Ichthyosaurs, like whales and dolphins were air-breathing and many experts believe the species were viviparous, as there have been many fossils containing fetuses. Ichthyosaurs had fin-like limbs, which were used to stabilize its body in the water and for directional control, as opposed to propulsion. They moved through the sea by using their large shark-like tail.

HOW THEY LOOKED

Early Ichthyosaurs were slender and lizard like. Only through a period of evolution did late Ichthyosaurs develop a dorsal fin, a tail fluke and were more fish shaped compared to their ancestors. An interesting point of mention is the look of later Ichthyosaurs. Although they looked like fish and had similar features such as a dorsal fin and tail fluke, they were not actually fishes. Many paleontologists note that later Ichthyosaurs are a good example of convergent evolution i.e., where similarities of structure are not from common ancestry.

In fact, during the early identification and reconstruction period of the ichthyosaur, the dorsal fin was omitted, as it had no skeletal structure. It was only when finely-preserved specimens were discovered in the 1890's in Germany, which revealed traces of the fin. Thanks to the unique preservation conditions of the site, paleontologists were able to excavate impressions of soft tissue, thereby changing the look of the dinosaur completely.

WHAT THEY ATE

For their food, many of the fish-shaped Ichthyosaurs relied heavily on marine life that shared some similarities to squids, called belemnites. Some early Ichthyosaurs had teeth specifically adapted to crushing shellfish. They also fed on a variety of different fish and some of the larger species had heavy jaws. This led to the assumption that such species would have fed on small reptiles along with fish and cephalopods.

PLESIOSAUR

Plesiosaurs were carnivorous, marine reptiles that lived from the Triassic to the Cretaceous periods. The species thrived in the sea for many years until the extinction level event during the middle Triassic period.

HOW THEY LOOKED

When first discovered, Plesiosaur fossils were fancifully said to have resembled a snake threaded through the shell of a turtle. The typical Plesiosaur had a broad body, a short tail and two pairs of large flippers. Plesiosaurs' four limb arrangement is thought to be an unusual one by experts and it is believed they used these flippers to propel themselves through the water. Plesiosaurs had no tail fin and the tail was most likely used to help control the animal's direction.

REPRODUCTION IN PLESIOSAURS

Originally it was believed that smaller species of Plesiosaurs would crawl onto land and lay their eggs. This theory seemed impossible, given how whales cannot survive being beached and even smaller Plesiosaurs were much larger than most whales. It was only in 1987, where evidence was discovered, indicating that Plesiosaurs were Viviparous.

DIET OF A PLESIOSAUR

When it came to the food source of Plesiosaurs, it varied depending on the long-necked and short-necked species.

Short-necked Plesiosaurs were apex predators in their respective foodwebs. They were pursuit-or-ambush predators with varying sizes of prey, and opportunistic feeders. Their teeth could have been used to pierce the bodies of fish. Their heads and teeth were very large, enabling them to grab and rip apart large prey.

Long-necked Plesiosaurs have been a topic of debate among experts for many years. There were three possible ways they fed, and these were based on the assumption that the neck was flexible. It was later discovered however, that the neck was actually rigid with limited vertical movement. This led to a number of new theories about how they could hunt. Some theories claim that they fed in a way similar to whales. Plesiosaurs did indeed have hundreds of teeth and could have used them like suspension feeders to sieve small Crustaceans from the water and filter out plankton.

What the Plesiosaur would have looked like.

QUICK FACTS

Viviparous means giving live birth, such as the case with whales giving birth to fully formed offspring.

The Extinction Level Event or ELE

The Cretaceous-Paleogene, more commonly called the (K-Pg) or (K-T) extinction was the sudden mass extinction of some three-fourths of plant and animal life on Earth, occurring nearly 66 million years ago.

Evidence for this extinction was first found in layers of rock that mark the boundary between the Cretaceous and Paleogene periods. Fossils that were once abundant did not appear in rocks after that time. Studies conducted on the fossils found between these two periods show that three out of every four plant and animals species went extinct at about the same time.

Artistic representation of the K-T extinction event from space.

IN PURSUIT OF ANSWERS

This led to a wide degree of speculation among scientists ranging from global plagues to supernovas frying the planet. It was only in 1980, that a team of researchers found an abundance of iridium deposits appearing alongside the K-Pg boundary. Iridium is a rare element in the Earth's crust but is abundant in space rocks and asteroids. This was the first piece of evidence that an asteroid caused the extinction but without a crater, the theory could not be confirmed.

Elsewhere, in the Mexican town of Chicxulub Puerto, oil company scientists discovered a crater late in the 1970's. They used variations in Earth's gravity to visualize the craters outline, reaching a size of 180 kilometers. Based on the size of the depressions, scientists estimated an asteroid hit the planet with ten billion times more energy than the nuclear bomb dropped on Hiroshima in 1945.

Evidence of the crater was further proof that a large asteroid did impact Earth. However, it was difficult to imagine how the asteroid could have led to the worldwide extinction of so many species. Later studies indicate that the blast was the trigger for an extinction level event (later called ELE).

The Chicxulub crater in the Yucatan Peninsula in Mexico

FALLOUT FROM THE IMPACT

When the asteroid collided with Earth, powerful gusts of winds roiled the atmosphere, debris rained from the sky, soot and dust scattered all across, leading to wildfires. That soot and dust then spread, casting a giant shadow over the planet.

According to computer models of the event, the darkness lasted so long and was so severe, it caused the planet to cool down. This simulation was created by first estimating the climate before the impact. Researchers determined what the climate was like from evidence of ancient plants and atmospheric carbon dioxide. Scientists also estimated a total of 70 billion metric tons of soot was floating in the air, blocking the sun.

For two years, no light reached the Earth's surface. Temperatures across the planet fell by 16 degrees, causing Arctic ice to spread southward. Some areas would have been hit hard by this change. Areas like the Pacific Ocean and near the equator would experience nosedives in temperature. This difference in temperature also explains why some species were able to survive the impact while others died off.

In 2016, a scientific drilling project obtained deep rock-core samples from the area around the Chicxulub impact crater. The findings here confirmed that the event was almost immediately followed by a mega tsunami, capable of bringing entire landmasses under water.

Evidence of this period of darkness can be found in fossils. Fossilized remains of lipid molecules in ancient microbes provide a temperature accord, according to some researchers. The cold darkness was the primary reason why many of the dinosaurs were wiped out. However, other planetary changes led to the demise of the dinosaurs.

QUICK FACTS

In geography, a pair of points antipodal to each other are situated such that, a straight line connecting the two would pass through Earth's center.

DECCAN TRAPS

Located in the Deccan Plateau of west-central India lie the Deccan traps, a large igneous province and is one of the largest volcanic features on Earth. When the traps began forming at the end of the Cretaceous period, the bulk of the volcanic eruption occurred some 66 million years ago followed by a series of eruptions, lasting 30000 years.

The release of volcanic gases, during the formation was also a contributing factor to climate change. Because of the magnitude of such a change, scientists speculate that the gases released during this formation played a role in the K-T extinction event. According to the prevailing theory, the sudden cooling caused by sulfurous volcanic gases and toxic gas emissions may have significantly contributed to mass extinctions, albeit at a slower pace. Studies published by scientists over the years speculate the Chicxulub impact could have exacerbated or induced the release of gases in the Deccan traps, due to the events occurring at antipodes.

While the event saw the demise of 75% of the world's population, it also provided some evolutionary opportunities. In its wake, the surviving animals underwent a remarkable adaptive radiation, resulting in sudden and prolific divergence into new forms and species within the empty ecological niches. Mammals in particular, diversified during the Paleogene period, which was part of the Cenozoic era.

Deccan traps, India

Life after extinction: The Cenozoic Era

The Cenozoic era is the current and most recent of the three Phanerozoic geological eras. It is also called the Age of Mammals. The Cenozoic is divided into three periods: the Paleogene, Neogene and Quaternary and seven epochs; the Paleocene, Eocene, Oligocene, Miocene, Pliocene, Pleistocene and Holocene. The Earth's climate had begun a drying and cooling trend, culminating in the glaciations of the Pleistocene Epoch and partially offset by the Paleocene-Eocene Thermal Maximum.

PALEOGENE PERIOD

The Paleogene period spans the extinction of non-avian dinosaurs to the dawn of the Neogene period. It features three epochs: Paleocene, Eocene and Oligocene. The Paleocene epoch was a transitional point between the K-T event to the jungle environment characterizing the Eocene. During this time, the Earth began to recover and continents were separated from each other. The Paleocene saw a rise in temperature, with jungles even reaching the poles. Archaic mammals such as Creodonts began filling the world in the absence of dinosaurs.

Drawing of what a Creodont would have looked like.

The Eocene epoch saw species in dense forests unable to evolve into larger forms. There was nothing over the weight of 10 kilograms. Among these species were early primates, whales, horses and many other early mammals. At the top of the food chain were birds like the Paracrax. Following a disruption in ocean currents worldwide, the world began to cool and jungles began to shrink. This change allowed mammals to reach mammoth proportions. Eocene also saw the rebirth of seasons.

The Oligocene epoch saw the expansion of grass, which in turn led to many new species to evolve. These species were the first elephants, cats, dogs, marsupials and many other species seen today. Thanks to the changing climate and seasonal rains, mammals continued to grow larger and larger.

NEOGENE PERIOD

The Neogene period spans from 23.03 million to 2.58 million years ago. It features two epochs: the Miocene epoch and the Pliocene epoch.

The Miocene epoch was when grass spread further, becoming the dominant plant in the world, taking over much of the forest area. Kelp forests evolved, encouraging the evolution of new species such as sea otters. During this time, Perissodactyla thrived and evolved into many different varieties and apes evolved into 30 species. Nearly 95% of all modern seed plants evolved during the mid-Miocene epoch.

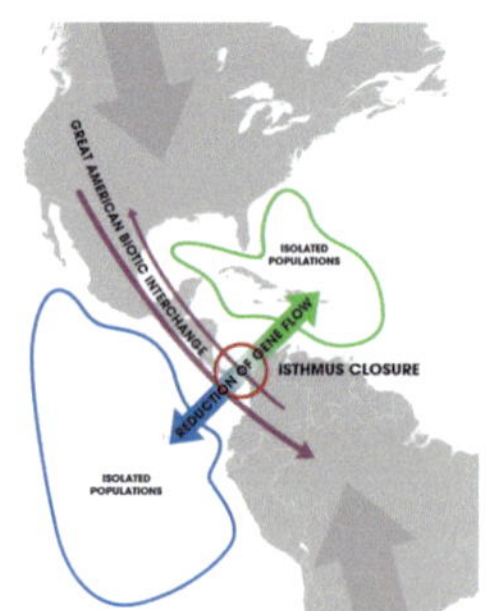

Geographical location of the Isthmus of Panama

The Pliocene epoch lasted from 5.333 million to 2.58 million years ago. This epoch saw dramatic climate changes, which led to the modern species of flora and fauna. Due to the ice ages reducing sea levels, the Mediterranean Sea dried up for a few million years. Australopithecus evolved in Africa, beginning the human branch. The isthmus of Panama formed, allowing for migration between north and south America. Climatic changes brought about the spread of savannas across the world, the deserts in Central Asia, the Indian monsoon and the beginning of the Sahara Desert. By this time, the world map had taken its present shape with only a few changes brought about in the Quaternary period.

QUATERNARY PERIOD

The Quaternary period covers 2.58 million years to present day and is the shortest geological period in the Phanerozoic Eon. The period saw modern animals and more dramatic changes to climate. It is divided into the Pleistocene epoch and the Holocene epoch.

The Pleistocene epoch ranged from 2.58 million years ago to 11,700 years ago. This period is more commonly known as the ice age thanks to the resulting cooling trend that began way back in the Mid-Eocene epoch. Africa in particular experienced a trend of desiccation resulting in the creation of the Sahara, Namib and Kalahari deserts. It was at this time many familiar animals evolved, which include mammoths, wolves, giant ground sloths, saber toothed cats and Homo sapiens. 100,000 years ago, saw the end of the worst droughts in Africa and led to the expansion of primitive humans. Nearing the end of the Pleistocene epoch, a major extinction wiped out much of the world's megafauna, including a few hominid species like the Neanderthals. The ice age affected all the continents, but Africa to a lesser extent. Many animals like the hippo survived through the ice age.

Following this, the Holocene Epoch began and lasts to the present day. All recorded history and the history of the world lies within the Holocene epoch.

Depictions of dinosaurs: Early period to present

For reasons that can perhaps only be explained by psychologists, dinosaurs have always had a large appeal among the general populace. This is seen by them being the subject of various books, comics, movies, television shows, web pages, toys, models and works of art in nearly every part of the world. Recognition of this pervasive celebration is due in no small part to the depictions of dinosaurs in popular media. Consequently, acknowledgement of mainstream influences, particularly in works of fiction is warranted in order to correct or confirm a number of commonly held notions about dinosaurs.

Sir Arthur Conan Doyle

Edgar Rice Burroughs

Dinosaurs were first portrayed relatively not long after their scientific descriptions in the early to mid-thirteenth century. The first mention of dinosaurs comes from Charles Dickens' book, Bleak House, in 1853, only 29 years after dinosaurs were recognized as a separate species. Other uses of dinosaurs in fiction remained relatively uncommon till 1912, when Sir Arthur Conan Doyle published 'The Lost World.' In a brief description, the book dealt with the experiences of five explorers who discover the existence of live dinosaurs like the Megalosaurus and Iguanodon, in a remote location in South America.

Since then, there have been similar portrayals of modern dinosaurs in remote places found in books written from 1915 to 1944 by Edgar Rice Burroughs. Among the dinosaurs were favourites like the Stegosaurus and Triceratops. From the 1940's through to the present, science-fiction magazines and comic books have based many of their stories around the imaginative theme of humans in conflict with dinosaurs. There have been some writers who have tried to incorporate scientific knowledge about dinosaurs in their works. Some of the best examples of these attempts are Jurassic Park in 1990, the Lost World in 1995 and Raptor Red in 1996.

The long and successful use of dinosaurs as subjects in films goes back to 1925, the year in which The Lost World was made. The movie, based on the work of Sir Arthur Conan Doyle featured the Allosaurus, Tyrannosaurus, Triceratops and other Mesozoic animals as either groups or individuals. The portrayal of this assemblage was a big departure from a standard cinematic formula of having a single dinosaur responsible for all the on-screen action and violence.

Many other dinosaur movies have animals that superficially resemble some known dinosaur species or are exaggerated and embellished conglomerations based on various traits from several known dinosaurs. A good example of the latter type are the Godzilla films by Toho.

Skull of an Australopithecus

WHY ARE THEY SO POPULAR?

While the depictions of dinosaurs are often the result of speculation, and their image is sure to change as more is learned about them, there's no denying that dinosaurs have had a lasting appeal on people due to a variety of reasons. Why they are so popular is due to several reasons:

One major reason why they've become so popular is that children and adults can admire them and not accidentally run into a dinosaur walking through the street. A fully rendered velociraptor for example, in all its glory and hunger is rendered completely harmless because they are extinct.

Thanks to the new knowledge learned about dinosaurs everyday, it becomes easy for people to imagine, speculate and depict how some dinosaurs would look. It has led many people to imagine different looks for several dinosaurs as well as create new ones. Modern media is rife with dinosaurs, both factual and fictitious in nature, and both depictions are widely embraced by the public.

Much of the knowledge people have about dinosaurs came from mounted skeletons in museums. It is only through the advancement of technology that more visceral looking dinosaurs are appearing in popular media. Because most dinosaurs are so big and unfamiliar, their skeletons are large and imposing, becoming the subject of wonder and awe. It makes sense that when most children visit the museum, they head to the dinosaur exhibits to see the skeletons as that is more captivating than anything else.

Dinosaurs, in the end shaped the evolution of ancient mammalian ancestors, which skittered around for over 150 million years in a dinosaur-dominated world, but they have been a milestone for humans to gauge their own history and evolutionary success against. Without dinosaurs, it is safe to say humanity would not be where we are now.

PAST HELPING THE FUTURE

Many scientists across the world firmly believe there are many more lessons yet to be learned from dinosaurs, including ones about the shape of the future. By learning in greater detail about how dinosaurs and other organisms have responded to climate change and other species in the distant past, experts are able to outline the possible consequences of current ecological catastrophes. In essence, the past may very well be the key to the future.

A pair of Denversaurus skeletons posed in a museum.

Made in United States
Cleveland, OH
13 January 2025